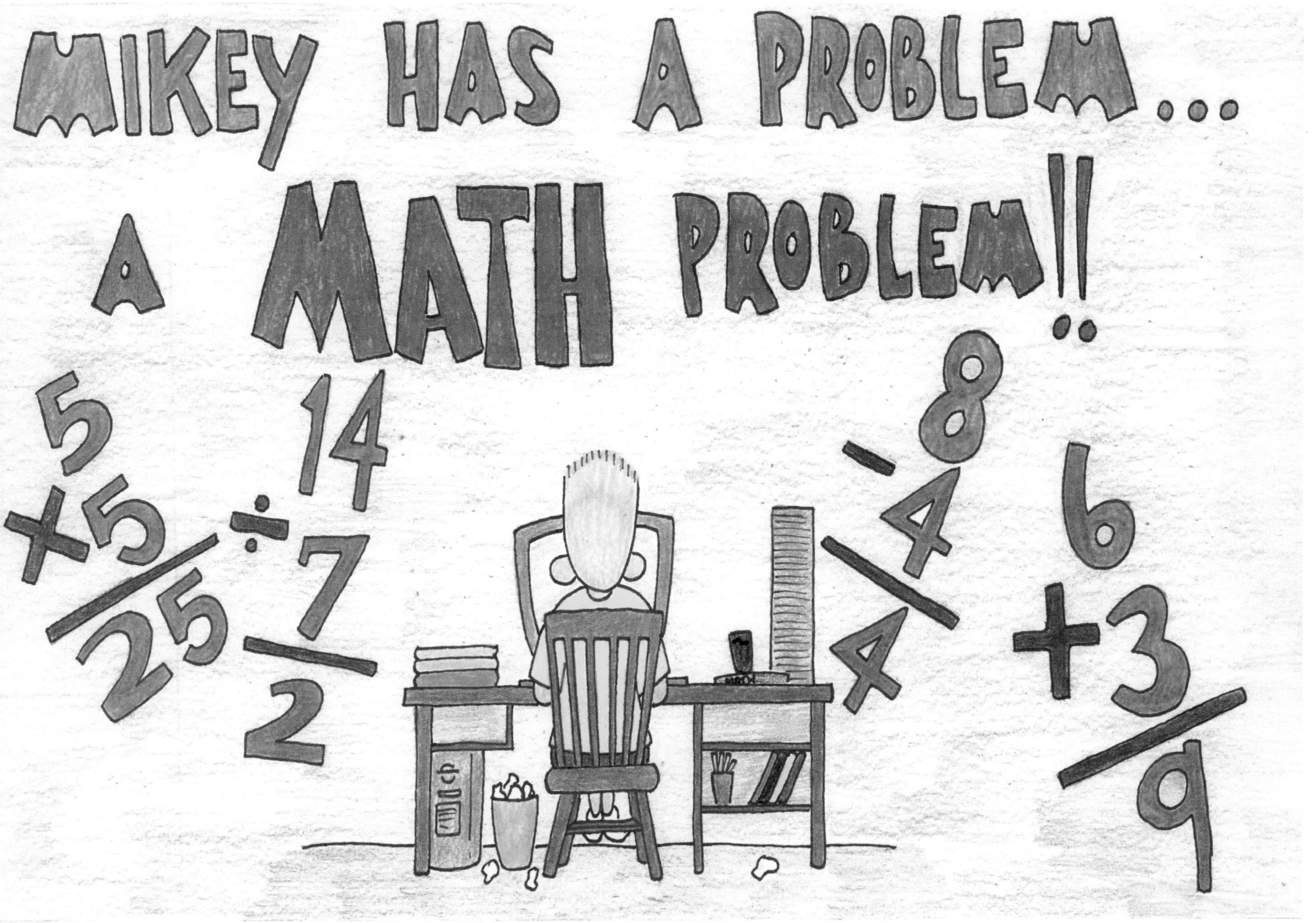
MIKEY HAS A PROBLEM...
A MATH PROBLEM!!
5
+5
25
14
÷7
2
8
-4
4
6
+3
9

"Read a book to a child and watch them smile for a moment....teach a child to read and watch them smile for a lifetime!!"

Michael Mota

Special Thanks

I would first like to thank my parents for always being there for me. They have been my inspiration throughout my life. I would also like to thank my editing staff for all their hard work, especially Dianne, Jane, and Kristine.

Published and Printed by:
  Lifevest Publishing
  8174 S. Holly Street #107
  Centennial, CO 80122
  www.lifevestpublishing.com

Printed in the United States of America

I.S.B.N. 1-932338-05-5

Dedication

I would like to dedicate this book to my fiancé, Dayna.
Without her there would be no "Mikey"!

By Michael Mota

Mikey has a problem... A MATH problem!

Mikey is a third grader at Gazoontight Elementary School. He likes school, but he hates math. Just the thought of math makes his stomach rumble. When it came to math class, Mikey would always be doing something else. Sometimes it would be counting the dots on the ceiling, and other times, it would be drawing on his desk. Anything was better than doing math, until Mikey's teacher decided to send a letter home. Mikey knew it was about his math grade, and he knew he was going to be in BIG trouble. His mother had told him time and time again, that if he didn't do well in math, he would have to be punished.

1+0=1

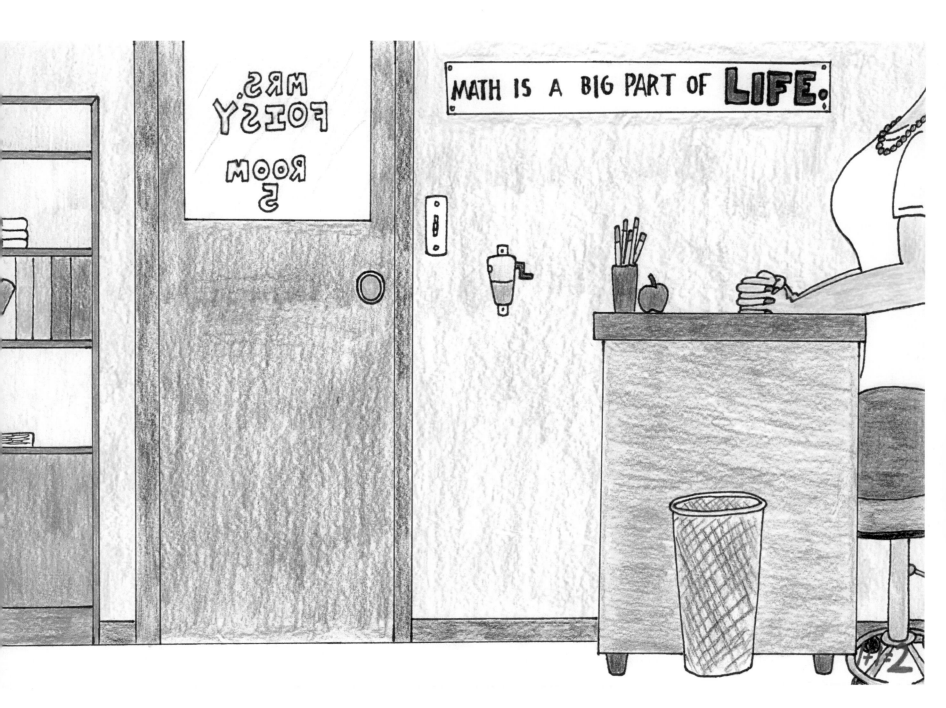

Well, the time had come for Mikey to face the music. His mother was in the kitchen washing dishes and his father was in the den.
"Mom, I have something for you from Mrs. Foisy; I think it's a letter."
His mother shut the water off and dried her hands. Mikey handed her the envelope and started quickly up the stairs to his room.

"Oh, no, you don't mister, you just sit right here," his mom instructed.

Mikey knew his life was over. No more games, no more friends, and definitely no more using his computer! Mikey watched his mother open and read the letter. He knew by the look on her face, how upset she was.

"Mikey, I can't believe you're failing your math class. Your father and I have asked you how you are doing every night. You never told us you were having problems."

"Mom, it's not that I have problems with math, it's just that I don't think it's important for me."

"So it's not that you can't do it, it's that you don't want to do it. Is that what you are telling me?"

"Exactly!"

Boy, that was the wrong thing to say. Mikey never saw his mother turn that color before. Mikey was sent to his room with no more games, no more going out with friends, and the thing that hurt Mikey the most, no more computer!

1+4=5

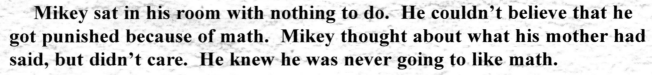

Mikey sat in his room with nothing to do. He couldn't believe that he got punished because of math. Mikey thought about what his mother had said, but didn't care. He knew he was never going to like math.

Mikey was so tired he fell right to sleep, but this wasn't going to be an ordinary sleep. Mikey was about to learn a lesson he would never, ever forget.

1+6=7

Mikey suddenly woke up. But he didn't wake up in his bed; he woke up in the woods. These weren't woods that Mikey had ever seen before. He began to scream at the top of his lungs, but it was of no use. The only thing he heard in return was his own voice echoing. He knew he was lost and he needed to find his way home, but where would he start?

Mikey decided to walk down a winding dirt path. There were so many trees that Mikey could barely see the sky. Mikey walked for hours and hours but all he could see was more trees. So, he stopped to rest for a few minutes. He hadn't eaten for hours and he was beginning to lose hope. Mikey then looked ahead and saw something that looked like a bridge, but like no other bridges Mikey had ever seen. The bridge was very long and very narrow. Then Mikey noticed a sign hanging on a gate at the bridge's entrance.

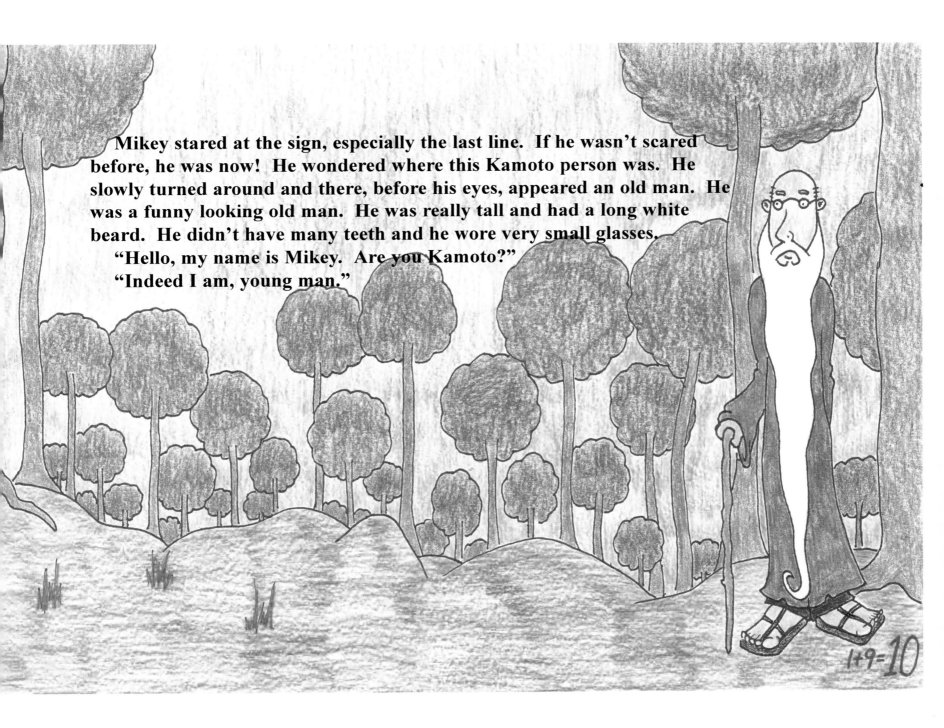

Mikey stared at the sign, especially the last line. If he wasn't scared before, he was now! He wondered where this Kamoto person was. He slowly turned around and there, before his eyes, appeared an old man. He was a funny looking old man. He was really tall and had a long white beard. He didn't have many teeth and he wore very small glasses.

"Hello, my name is Mikey. Are you Kamoto?"

"Indeed I am, young man."

1+9=10

Mikey wanted to laugh at the funny old man, but caught himself. He knew that the old man was the only one who could get him home.

"I am lost and I need to find my way home."

Kamoto answered, "You will need to cross this bridge, but before you can cross it, you will need to take a test. I know you don't like math, but this test will involve a math problem."

Mikey had nothing to say to Kamoto. He couldn't believe that Kamoto knew he didn't like math. He began to get really scared. If he had just liked math, then he would be able to cross the bridge and go home.

"Can I answer a different problem, anything but a math problem?" Mikey begged Kamoto.

"Sorry, my boy, it will have to be a math problem. And this is it..."

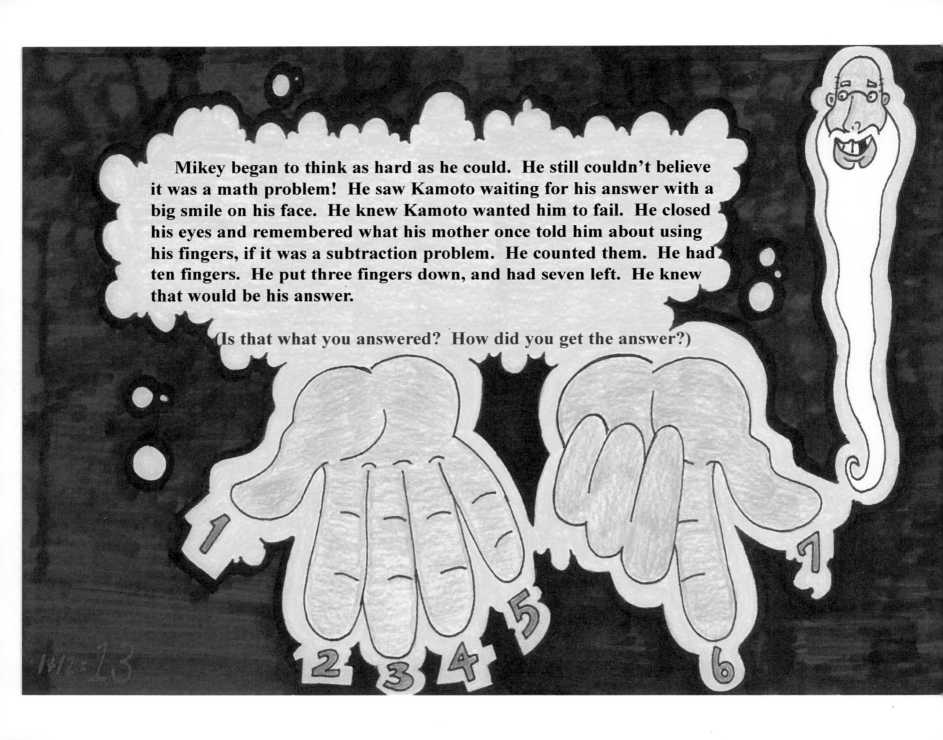

Mikey began to think as hard as he could. He still couldn't believe it was a math problem! He saw Kamoto waiting for his answer with a big smile on his face. He knew Kamoto wanted him to fail. He closed his eyes and remembered what his mother once told him about using his fingers, if it was a subtraction problem. He counted them. He had ten fingers. He put three fingers down, and had seven left. He knew that would be his answer.

(Is that what you answered? How did you get the answer?)

"Excuse me Kamoto, I have my answer. My answer is 7. There are 7 bridges left."

Kamoto's jaw dropped. He couldn't believe Mikey got the answer right.

"Very good, my boy! You may cross the bridge, but the problems only get more difficult from here on," Kamoto once again chuckled.

Kamoto was gone. He disappeared and the gate to the bridge suddenly opened. Mikey was able to cross the bridge. He was so happy, but he was nervous about the problems to come.

1+13=14

Mikey once again began his journey to find his way home. The woods were cluttering his head with all types of noises. He had traveled a long way again when he came upon a giant apple tree. He was starving from his long journey, so he decided to climb the tree and pick an apple. He walked up to the tree and just as he was about to climb it, Kamoto appeared once again.

"My dear boy, you must be starving."

"I am, I am," repeated Mikey a few more times.

"Well, if you want an apple, you know what you must do," said Kamoto.

Mikey knew what he must do.

1+14 = 15

This time, Mikey looked down at his hands and saw he only had ten fingers. He started to panic until he remembered what his mother had told him about subtracting higher numbers. He looked down at his feet and came up with an idea. If he had ten fingers and ten toes that would equal the amount of apples in the tree! He took away seven fingers and he had three fingers and ten toes left, so he knew the answer would be thirteen.

"I have my answer," Mikey said nervously to Kamoto. "My answer is 13."

"Why that is right my boy; you may eat as many apples as you would like, but beware, the problems on your journey home will become more difficult as you go on," warned Kamoto.

Suddenly, Kamoto was gone, and Mikey was left to eat his reward.

(Is that what you answered? How did you come up with your answer?)

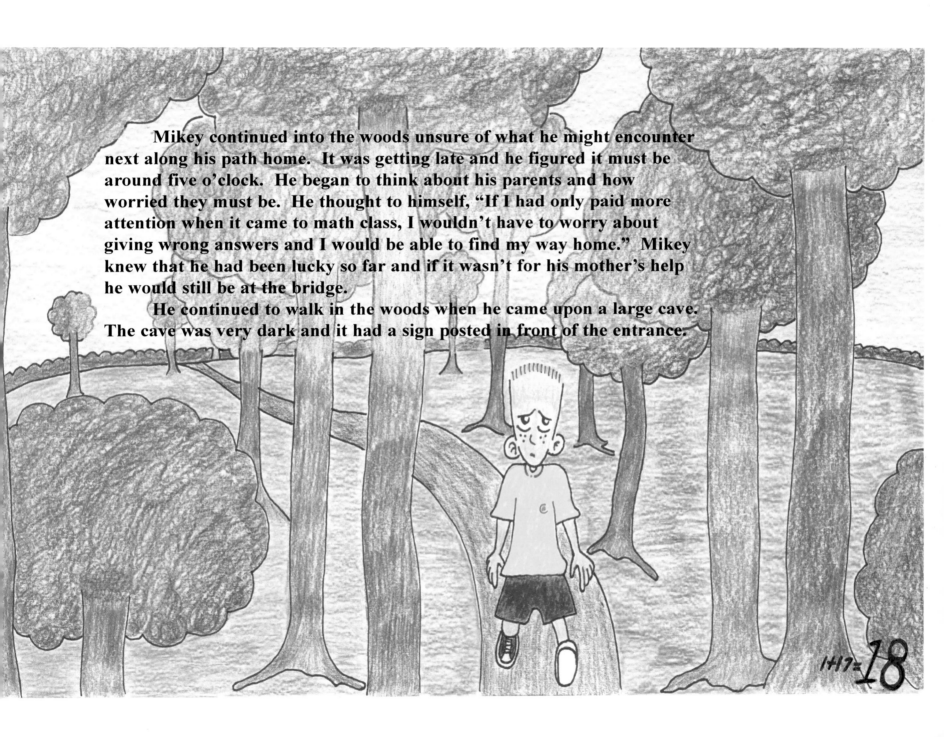

Mikey continued into the woods unsure of what he might encounter next along his path home. It was getting late and he figured it must be around five o'clock. He began to think about his parents and how worried they must be. He thought to himself, "If I had only paid more attention when it came to math class, I wouldn't have to worry about giving wrong answers and I would be able to find my way home." Mikey knew that he had been lucky so far and if it wasn't for his mother's help he would still be at the bridge.

He continued to walk in the woods when he came upon a large cave. The cave was very dark and it had a sign posted in front of the entrance.

1+17= 18

Mikey knew just by reading the sign that he was doomed. He began to scream as loud as he could, but was only answered once by the echo of his voice. Then he heard a loud laugh coming from inside the cave. So he called out to the voice and out came Kamoto.

"Why are you yelling, my boy?" Kamoto asked.

"I want to go home. I am so sorry I didn't pay attention in math class. I promise if you let me go home, I will learn to like math," Mikey begged.

HA! HA! HA! HA!

"I'm sorry my boy, but I can't do that. The only way home is to get all the problems correct. So far, you have answered all the problems! But this time the problem is much more difficult and you will need to think very hard."

Mikey began to cry, but it didn't bother Kamoto. He had seen many boys and girls get lost in these woods and he knew that not many had made it past the cave.

$1 + 20 = 21$

If thirty girls and twenty boys tried to enter the
cave and only ten girls and five boys made it in,
how many boys and girls were unable to enter and
were left outside the cave?

If you were Mikey, would you be able
to pass the cave?

Turn the page and find out.

1+21=22

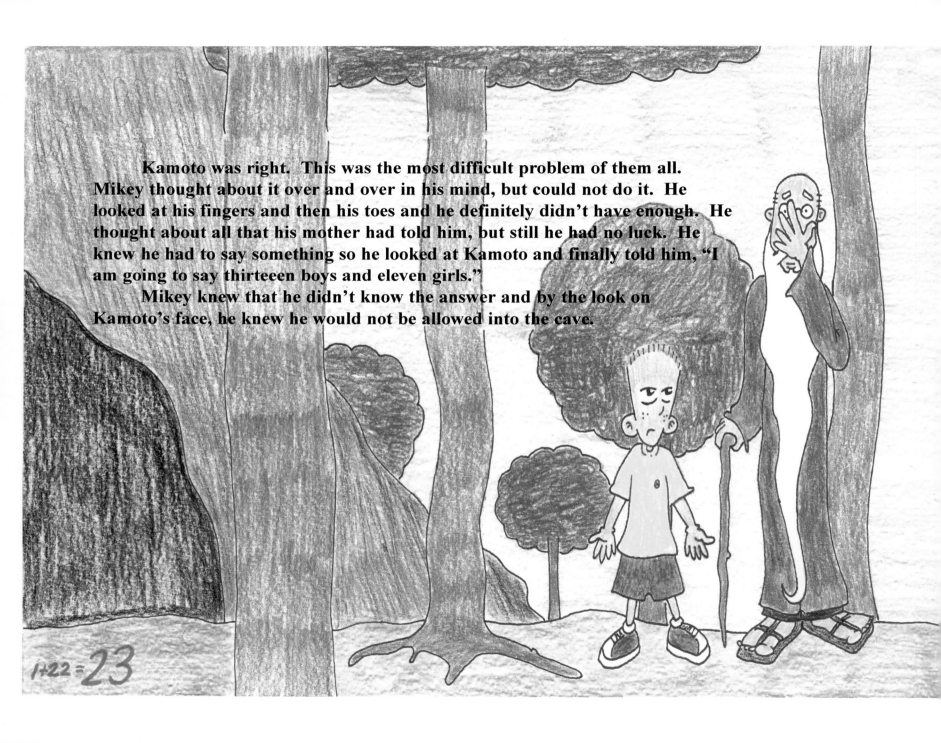

Kamoto was right. This was the most difficult problem of them all. Mikey thought about it over and over in his mind, but could not do it. He looked at his fingers and then his toes and he definitely didn't have enough. He thought about all that his mother had told him, but still he had no luck. He knew he had to say something so he looked at Kamoto and finally told him, "I am going to say thirteeen boys and eleven girls."

Mikey knew that he didn't know the answer and by the look on Kamoto's face, he knew he would not be allowed into the cave.

1+22 = 23

"My boy, I'm sorry, but I can not let you through. I told you that the problems would only get harder," said Kamoto.

"I am very sorry, Kamoto, but is there any way I might have another chance?"

"Well, my boy," Kamoto thought to himself and then said, "There is one other way, but..."

"But what?" Mikey said very eagerly.

$1 + 2^3 = 24$

"But the problem is even harder than this one. You must follow this dirt path and it will lead you to a waterfall. This will be your only chance to make it home."

Mikey was about to ask Kamoto another question, but Kamoto quickly vanished again. This was Mikey's last chance to make it home and he knew the problem would be the most difficult thus far.

(20 girls and 15 boys were not allowed to enter the cave. Did you answer the problem correctly? How did you answer it? What did Mikey do wrong?)

1+24=25

Mikey ran down the dirt road and came to the waterfall that Kamoto had described. It was the most beautiful thing he had ever seen. He had read about them in books and had even seen one in the movies. It was a magnificent waterfall. It stretched the whole length of the woods. He couldn't see anything but water on both sides. There was no way to cross the waterfall because it was too high to climb and too deep to swim. The only way across was through it and that wasn't possible. So he decided to get as close as he could to the waterfall. Mikey couldn't believe his eyes. He thought he was still sleeping because when he looked through the waterfall he could see his house on the other side! He saw his mother and father in the yard and his sister riding her bike. He tried to yell to them, but there was no response.

Then he reached down and grabbed some rocks to throw, but that didn't work either. He could see them, but they couldn't see him. It couldn't get any worse for Mikey. He was so close to home, but yet so far. How could he possibly get across? Mikey began to look around for a sign and sure enough, posted on a tree was a sign.

Nothing could prepare Mikey for how badly he felt. He knew if he didn't answer this problem correctly, he would be stuck in the woods forever. Just as he started to look over his shoulder, Kamoto appeared.

"Well, my boy, this is it. If you answer this problem wrong, you will be stuck with me in these woods forever. It's not that bad, we have a lot of things to do here," said Kamoto.

"Like what?" Mikey asked.

"Well, we have plenty of math problems we could do."

"Oh no, please let me go home, I promise..."

Just as Mikey was about to finish, he was interrupted by the final and most important problem.

1+27=28

Mikey began to think about the problem as hard as he could. He knew it was hopeless trying to answer this problem. Kamoto was right! He would be stuck in the woods forever. But Mikey needed to try to answer the question as best as he could. He looked around and gathered some rocks and he used them to represent the ten countries. Then he looked around for twigs and used them as rainbows. He put two twigs next to each rock. But when he came to the sixth rock, he ran out of twigs. He ran around the woods in search of more twigs but, alas, he had no luck.

1+29? 30

"I need to know your answer," Kamoto said.

"Can I have a few more minutes?" Mikey asked. "I think I may be able to answer this one correctly."

"I'm sorry my boy, I need an answer right now."

Mikey counted the twigs he had sitting next to each rock. Then he tried to guess how many more twigs he would need to solve the problem.

"My answer is eighteen rainbows."

Mikey was so nervous that he closed his eyes while he waited for the answer.

"I'm sorry Mikey, but the answer is twenty rainbows. You were very close, but it looks like you will be stuck with me forever."

(Did you answer the problem correctly? How did you answer it? What did Mikey do wrong?)

1+30=31

As soon as Mikey was about to beg Kamoto to let him go home, Kamoto had disappeared once again. The only thing left was a large sign standing in place of Kamoto.

The next sound Mikey heard was his mother's voice saying,
"Mikey wake up! You are having a dream."
"Where am I? Where is Kamoto? And the rainbow, and...?"
"What are you talking about Mikey? Calm down, it was only a dream. Now get ready for school. I hope you do better in that math class of yours and try to bring up your math grade."

Mikey could not believe his eyes. He was in his own bed, in his own room, in his own house. It may have been a dream, but Mikey would never forget Kamoto.

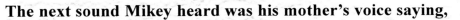

ABOUT THE AUTHOR

Michael Mota is a 22 year old elementary school teacher who lives in North Providence, Rhode Island. He loves to teach and work with children everyday. It has been Michael's dream to write a children's book. He decided to write this book to not only tell a great story, but to also give teachers and parents a tool to help their children with problem solving. He hopes to write a series of educational books.

ABOUT THE ILLUSTRATOR

Michael Soares is 23 years old and also lives in North Providence, Rhode Island. Ever since Michael was young he has always had a passion to draw. He was very excited to have the opportunity to illustrate this book. He hopes to continue the series.

To Order Copies of
Mikey Has A Problem

ISBN 1-932338-05-5

You may order online at:
www.lifevestpublishing.com/mikey.htm

by phone at:
303-221-1007

by mail:
Just send check or money order to:
Lifevest Publishing
8174 S. Holly Street #107
Centennial, CO 80122